Mud Puddle

Story by Robert Munsch
Illustrations by Sami Suomalainen

Annick Press Ltd.
Toronto • New York • Vancouver

Seventh printing, revised edition, May 2004

We acknowledge the support of the Canada Council for the Arts, the Ontario Arts
Council, and the Government of Canada through the Book Publishing Industry
Development Program (BPIDP) for our publishing activities.

Cataloging in Publication Data
　Munsch, Robert N., 1945 -
　　Mud puddle

(Munsch for kids)
Rev. ed.
ISBN 1-55037-469-9 (bound) ISBN 1-55037-468-0 (pbk.)

I. Suomalainen, Sami. II. Title. III. Series: Munsch, Robert N., 1945-
Munsch for kids.

PS8576.U575M8 1995　jC813'.54　C95-931712-0
PZ7.M85Mu 1995

Distributed in Canada by:　　Published in the U.S.A. by Annick Press (U.S.) Ltd.
Firefly Books Ltd.　　　　　　Distributed in the U.S.A. by:
66 Leek Crescent　　　　　　　Firefly Books (U.S.) Inc.
Richmond Hill, ON　　　　　　 P.O. Box 1338
L4B 1H1　　　　　　　　　　　Ellicott Station
　　　　　　　　　　　　　　　Buffalo, NY 14205

Printed and bound in Canada
by Friesens, Altona, Manitoba.

visit us at: **www.annickpress.com**

To Jeffrey—R.M.

To my wife, June—S.S.

Jule Ann's mother bought her clean new clothes.

Jule Ann put on a clean new shirt and buttoned it up the front. She put on clean new pants and buttoned them up the front. Then she walked outside and sat down under the apple tree.

Unfortunately, hiding up in the apple tree, there was a mud puddle. It saw Jule Ann sitting there and it jumped right on her head.

She got completely all over muddy. Even her ears were full of mud.

Jule Ann ran inside yelling, "Mummy, Mummy! A Mud Puddle jumped on me."

Her mother picked her up, took off all her clothes and dropped her into a tub of water. She scrubbed Jule Ann till she was red all over.

She washed out her ears.

She washed out her eyes.

She even washed out her mouth.

Jule Ann put on a clean new shirt and buttoned it up the front. She put on clean new pants and buttoned them up the front. Then she looked out the back door. She couldn't see a mud puddle anywhere, so she walked outside and sat down in her sand box.

The sand box was next to the house and hiding up on top of the house there was a mud puddle.

It saw Jule Ann sitting down there and it jumped right on her head. She got completely all over muddy. Even her nose was full of mud.

Jule Ann ran inside yelling, "Mummy, Mummy! A Mud Puddle jumped on me."

Jule Ann's mother picked her up, took off all her clothes and dropped her into a tub of water. She scrubbed Jule Ann till she was red all over.

She washed out her ears.
She washed out her eyes.
She washed out her mouth.
She even washed out her nose.

Jule Ann put on a clean new shirt and buttoned it up the front. Then she put on clean new pants and buttoned them up the front. Then she had an idea. She reached way back in the closet and got a big yellow raincoat. She put it on and walked outside. There was no mud puddle anywhere, so she yelled, "Hey, Mud Puddle!"

Nothing happened, so she yelled, even louder, "Hey, Mud Puddle!!"

Jule Ann was standing in the sunshine in her raincoat, getting very hot. She pulled back her hood.

Nothing happened. She took off her raincoat.

As soon as she took off her coat, out from behind the dog house, there came the mud puddle.

It ran across the grass and jumped right on Jule Ann's head.

She got completely all
over muddy. Jule Ann ran
inside yelling, "Mummy,
Mummy! A Mud Puddle
jumped on me."

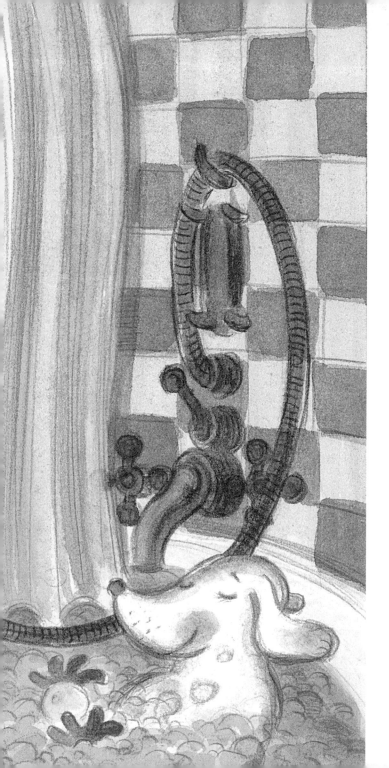

Her mother picked her up, took off all her clothes and dropped her into a tub full of water. She scrubbed Jule Ann till she was red all over.

She washed out her ears.
She washed out her eyes.
She washed out her mouth.
She washed out her nose.
She even washed out her belly button.

Jule Ann put on a clean new shirt and buttoned it up the front. She put on clean new pants and buttoned them up the front. Then she sat beside the back door because she was afraid to go outside.

Then she had an idea.

She reached up to the sink and took a bar of smelly yellow soap. She gave it a smell – yecch! She took another bar of smelly yellow soap and gave it a smell – yecch! She put the smelly yellow soap in her pockets. Then she ran out into the middle of the back yard and yelled, "Hey, Mud Puddle!"

The mud puddle jumped over the fence and ran right toward her.

Jule Ann threw a bar of soap right into the mud puddle's middle. The mud puddle stopped.

Jule Ann threw the other bar of soap right into the mud puddle. The mud puddle said, "Awk, yecch, wackh!"

It ran across the grass, jumped over the fence, and never came back.

Other books in the Munsch for Kids series: